Teggs is no ordinary dinosaur –
he's an **ASTROSAUR!** Captain of
the amazing spaceship DSS *Sauropod*,
he goes on dangerous missions and
fights evil – along with his faithful
crew, Gipsy, Arx and Iggy.

For more astro-fun visit the website
www.astrosaurs.co.uk

Astrosaurs

THE SPACE GHOSTS

Steve Cole

Illustrated by Woody Fox

RED FOX

THE SPACE GHOSTS
A RED FOX BOOK 978 1 849 41154 7

First published in Great Britain by Red Fox,
an imprint of Random House Children's Books
A Random House Group Company

First Red Fox edition published, 2006
This Red Fox edition published, 2010

1 3 5 7 9 10 8 6 4 2

The Random House Group Limited supports the Forest Stewardship Council
(FSC), the leading international forest certification organization. All our titles that
are printed on Greenpeace-approved FSC-certified paper carry the FSC logo. Our
paper procurement policy can be found at www.rbooks.co.uk/environment.

Typeset in Bembo MT Schoolbook 16/20pt
by Falcon Oast Graphic Art Ltd.

Red Fox Books are published by Random House Children's Books,
61–63 Uxbridge Road, London W5 5SA

www.**kids**at**randomhouse**.co.uk
www.**rbooks**.co.uk

Addresses for companies within The Random House Group Limited can be found
at: www.randomhouse.co.uk/offices.htm

THE RANDOM HOUSE GROUP Limited Reg. No. 954009

A CIP catalogue record for this book is available from the British Library.

Printed and bound in Great Britain by CPI Bookmarque, Croydon, CR0 4TD

For Jack and Oliver Greenwood

WARNING!

THINK YOU KNOW ABOUT DINOSAURS?

THINK AGAIN!

The dinosaurs ...

Big, stupid, lumbering reptiles. Right?

All they did was eat, sleep and roar a bit. Right?

Died out millions of years ago when a big meteor struck the Earth. Right?

Wrong!

The dinosaurs weren't stupid. They may have had small brains, but they used them well. They had big thoughts and big dreams.

By the time the meteor hit, the last dinosaurs had already left Earth for ever. Some breeds had discovered how to travel through space as early as the Triassic period, and were already enjoying a new life among the stars. No one has found evidence of dinosaur technology yet. But the first fossil bones were only unearthed in 1822, and new finds are being made all the time.

The proof is out there, buried in the ground.

And the dinosaurs live on, way out in space, even now. They've settled down in a place they call the Jurassic Quadrant and over the last sixty-five million years they've gone on evolving.

 The dinosaurs we'll be meeting are part of a special group called the Dinosaur Space Service. Their job is to explore space, to go on exciting missions and to fight evil and protect the innocent!

These heroic herbivores are not just dinosaurs.

They are *astrosaurs*!

NOTE: The following story has been translated from secret Dinosaur Space Service records. Earthling dinosaur names are used throughout, although some changes have been made for easy reading. There's even a guide to help you pronounce the dinosaur names on the next page.

Talking Dinosaur!

How to say the prehistoric
names in this book . . .

STEGOSAURUS – *STEG-oh-SORE-us*

TRICERATOPS – *try-SERRA-tops*

IGUANODON – *ig-WA-noh-don*

HADROSAUR – *die-MORF-oh-don*

TRICERATOPS – *HAD-roh-sore*

DIPLODOCUS – *di-PLOH-doh-kus*

KENTROSAURUS – *KEN-troh-SORE-us*

DIMORPHODON – *die-MORF-oh-don*

VELOCIRAPTOR – *vel-O-si-RAP-tor*

THE CREW OF THE DSS SAUROPOD

**CAPTAIN
TEGGS STEGOSAUR**

ARX ORANO,
FIRST OFFICER

GIPSY SAURINE,
COMMUNICATIONS
OFFICER

IGGY TOOTH,
CHIEF ENGINEER

Jurassic Quadrant

Ankylos

Steggos

Diplox

INDEPENDE
DINOSAU
ALLIANC

vegetarian sector

Squawk
Major

DSS
UNION OF
PLANETS

PTEROSAURIA

Tri System

Corytho

Lambeos

Aqua Minor

Iguanos

Geldos Cluster

Teerex
Major

Olympus

lanet Sixty

TYRANNOSAUR
TERRITORIES

carnivore
sector

Raptos

THEROPOD EMPIRE

Cryptos

Megalos

vegmeat
zone

(neutral space)

A REPTILE
SPACE

Pliosaur
Nurseries

Not to scale

THE SPACE
GHOSTS

Chapter One

THE CURSED TREASURE

 The shuttle swooped out of the night sky, like a metal egg falling from a nest of stars. It zoomed over the surface of a barren planet. The landscape was lit by a dozen silver moons, but the view was rotten. There was no sign of life. No trees or rivers. Nothing but rocks, slowly crumbling to dust.

The shuttle landed and Captain Teggs Stegosaur, an orange-brown stegosaurus, stuck out his inquisitive beak.

"So this is the planet Creepus," he said. Teggs was a captain in the Dinosaur Space Service. He looked up at the sky where his amazing ship, the DSS *Sauropod*, hung like an extra-shiny star. It was warm and snug and safe up there. Down here, it was cold and  creepy. The wind howled. Stone and shingle scrunched beneath his four feet. Anything could be hiding in the caves and canyons of this lonely world.

Teggs smiled to himself. It was just the sort of place for an adventure!

A triceratops followed him out of the shuttle. This was Arx, Teggs's trusty first

4

officer. "Not a nice place for a picnic," he noted, ducking his large frilly head as the wind blew sand in his eyes. "Luckily, Camp Kentro is not far from here."

"I landed the shuttle as close as I could," said Iggy, scampering after him. He was a stocky iguanodon who had been in a fight or two, and he was a brilliant engineer. "It's not my fault this old camp has no landing pad!"

"It's OK," said Teggs. "The walk will do us good."

"I've got the tracker," called Gipsy Saurine. This stripy duckbill looked after the *Sauropod*'s

communications. As she stepped out to join her crewmates, the tracker on her wrist was already bleeping. "This will lead us straight to Camp Kentro."

"Where Shanta and his diplodocus crew will be waiting to give us a nice cup of swamp tea," said Arx. "I hope!"

They set off through the stinging wind, and Teggs thought about their mission. Shanta Digg was a famous diplodocus miner. He and his team had worked in mines all across the Jurassic Quadrant. They had dug for diamonds on Diplox. They had rummaged for rubies on Raxas Four. And they had come here to Creepus in search of something very special indeed . . .

But they had found only problems. Shanta had called the DSS for help, and Admiral Rosso, the head of the DSS, had sent the *Sauropod* straight here. But so far, no one had told Teggs exactly what was wrong. All Rosso would say was that it was "a delicate matter".

What help did the miners need?

After trudging through the wilderness for several minutes, Teggs saw some battered buildings in the valley below. They looked old and deserted in the silvery moonlight – and extremely spooky.

Gipsy checked her tracker. "That must be Camp Kentro."

"Why is it called that?" wondered Iggy.

Arx, who was very brainy, shouted to him over the wind. "Fifty years ago, some kentrosaurus miners came to Creepus. This was where they set up their camp."

"Why would a load of diplodocus want to stay in this old place?" asked Gipsy.

"Come on!" Teggs charged off towards the bundle of old buildings. "Let's go and ask them!"

A few minutes later they reached the camp. Iggy jabbed his thumb spike on the doorbell.

"Who's there?" a voice whispered.

"Captain Teggs and his fellow astrosaurs!" said Teggs.

A minute later the door slid open. A sleek head the size of a rugby ball pushed out

at them, waving about on the end of a
neck as thick as a tree and as long as
a ladder.

Teggs recognized the diplodocus at
once. "Shanta Digg?"

"Aye, my lad," said Shanta, looking
about nervously. "That's me. Now,
come inside, quick. And close the door
behind you!"

Arx frowned. "He seems a bit jittery."

"Yes, what's up, Shanta?" said Iggy,
walking inside. "You look like you've
seen a ghost."

"Ghost?" cried
Shanta. He banged
his head on the
ceiling in surprise and
started to stammer.
"W-w-what ghost?
Where?"

"Nowhere!" said
Gipsy. "It was just a
figure of speech."

"F-f-figure? *What* figure?" The whole camp shook as he stamped around and around in a tizzy. "Plod, quick! There's another figure!"

"Not *another* one!" Plod, a slightly larger diplodocus, swung her neck round the corner. She was older and greyer than Shanta but no less frightened. "Where is it? What was it doing? Who—?"

"There's no one here but us!" yelled Teggs. His sudden outburst stopped the two diplodocus in their tracks. "Now, what is going on around here?"

Shanta looked a little bit calmer now. "Sorry, folks," he said. "We're all a bit on edge." He nodded his head at the older dinosaur. "This is Plod, my assistant. She runs the base here – and she's also the toughest miner this side of the Vegmeat Zone!"

"Pleased to meet you," said Teggs, and he introduced his crew. "Now, what has been going on here?"

"Come through to the crew room," said Plod. "We'll tell you all about it . . ."

Gipsy noticed that the diplodocus had to stoop and squash together as they plodded through the old, cracked corridors. "It's a bit of a squeeze for you, isn't it?"

"The people who built this camp were much smaller than us," Plod agreed as she started to prepare a snack in the crew-room kitchen. "Your captain looks a lot like them."

"A kentrosaurus is a type of stegosaur," Teggs said brightly. "You could say we're distant relatives."

"Aye, well. We had our own base, but it was squashed by a landslide," Shanta explained. "Most of the lads are staying on our ship over there. But me, Plod and a couple more decided to stay here and look for clues!"

"Clues for what?" asked Iggy.

"Clues that the kentrosaurus may have left behind . . ." Shanta dipped down his head to get a better look at Iggy. "Clues to something that will make us the richest dinosaurs in space!"

Teggs felt a tingle travel down his tail. "Well? What is it?"

12

"We think they found something in the ground here," said Plod. "The most precious crystals in the universe – pure *dispium*."

"Dispium? Also known as the cursed treasure?" Arx chuckled. "That's just an old miner's tale, a legend. There is no such stuff."

"There is too!" said Shanta hotly. "It looks like little glass cubes, all aglow with a dark fire."

Arx looked doubtful. "So the old stories say."

"They're not stories, they're *true!*" Shanta insisted.

"Grub up!" announced Plod. She handed them each a cup of swamp tea and a plate of fried ferns.

Teggs swallowed both down in a single gulp. "Ugh . . . !" he spluttered. They tasted dreadful!

"Sorry," said Plod. "We're miners, not cooks!"

Teggs smiled weakly. "Tell us about this cursed treasure."

"Dispium crystals are said to have many mysterious powers," said Shanta.

"Like what?" asked Iggy.

Plod shrugged. "We don't know exactly. Anyone who's ever discovered dispium has soon disappeared without a trace. Including the miners who built this camp fifty years ago!"

Gipsy's eyes grew wider. "But . . . I thought the kentrosaurus simply left this place behind when they went back home?"

"They never *did* go back home," said Shanta. "Their ship disappeared. And no trace was ever found of the miners . . . until now."

Teggs was puzzled. "So, where are they?"

"Right here," Plod whispered, her black eyes wide and afraid. "Haunting us!"

Iggy gulped. "*Haunting* you?"

"The kentrosaurus are ghosts," said Shanta quietly. "They found the cursed treasure, all right. And this is their terrible fate — to haunt the planet Creepus for ever!"

Chapter Two

THE VISITOR IN THE NIGHT

The astrosaurs looked at one another
nervously. A fierce storm was now
raging outside. The wind howled like
an animal in pain. It sent a shiver
through them all.

Teggs knew now why Admiral Rosso had called this a delicate matter. Had the miners gone nutty, or were they being haunted for real? "So you believe you have seen ghosts here?"

"Many times." Shanta shivered. "They come out of the darkness and the shadows, all aglow. Rear up in front of us. Swish their tails about. You can see right through them!"

"No wonder you seemed so scared before," Gipsy murmured.

"We thought the tales of the curses and people disappearing were just silly stories," said Plod. "We would never have come if we had known the truth!"

"Well, I don't believe in ghosts," Arx declared. "I'm sure there's another explanation for what you're seeing. Perhaps it's a trick of the light?"

"They only come when it's dark," whispered Plod.

"And there are lots of dark corners in this old camp, my lad," Shanta warned him.

Thunder rumbled outside, and lightning flashed at the windows. The wind blew ever harder.

Teggs cleared his throat. "Well, it's getting late, and it was a long journey here. Perhaps we should go to bed and talk about this in the morning? Nothing seems as scary in daylight."

Shanta nodded. "Aye. Plod will show you to your rooms. Sleep well, folks. I hope there are no . . . *interruptions*."

Iggy gulped. "Me too!"

Plod led the astrosaurs through to Camp Kentro's sleeping block. The rooms were dusty and smelled like old cupboards. Gipsy stuck her head inside one and sneezed.

"I bet no one's been in here for – well, fifty years!"

"Sorry," said Plod gruffly. "We're miners, not cleaners. We enjoy a bit of dirt and dust and discomfort. In fact, I can't sleep anywhere that's cosy and clean!"

There was a sudden crash of thunder. The wind was blowing harder than ever. "Maybe I should open the window," Gipsy joked. "That would blow away some of the cobwebs!"

Teggs grinned. "And everything else besides!"

Iggy took the room opposite Gipsy's. "There are two more rooms free round the corner, at the far end of the corridor," Plod announced. Teggs and Arx said goodnight and she led them away.

Gipsy sighed. "Do *you* believe in ghosts, Iggy?"

"Of course not!" Iggy protested.

But then a strange clanking sound started up. Iggy got such a surprise he leaped straight into Gipsy's arms!

RATTA-TATTA-BZZZZZZZZZZ-CLUNK! went the noise.

Teggs and Arx came skidding back round the corner.

"What's happening?" asked Teggs. "What's that sound?"

Gipsy quickly put Iggy down. "I . . . I don't know!" She gulped. "I think it's coming from my room!"

"It's a ghost!" cried Iggy.

TATTA-RATTA-CLUNK-RATTA-BZZZZZZZZZZ!

"No, the ghosts are silent," Plod told him, peering round. "They don't make a sound. What you can hear are the toilets next to your room!"

Arx frowned. "Toilets? Making *that* dreadful noise?"

Iggy smiled. "Someone must have eaten well tonight!"

"It's the pipes, I think," said Plod. "They make that noise a lot. We don't know how to fix them – we're miners, not plumbers!"

"I'm quite good with a spanner," said Iggy. "I'll have it sorted out in no time!"

The astrosaurs said goodnight again, and Plod showed Arx and Teggs to their rooms.

Teggs looked round as he closed the door behind him. The room was dirty.

A pile of pickaxes and spades sat rusting in a corner. A faded picture was pinned up on the wall. It showed a pretty kentrosaurus girl with ribbons tied around the spikes on her back.

As he got into the dry, mossy bed, Teggs felt sad. Where was the girl in the picture now? After fifty years, was she still waiting for the long-lost miner to come home?

With a swish of his tail, he switched off the light. Muffled thumps and bumps floated through the wall. A ghost? No, just Arx getting ready for bed next door.

Teggs smiled and squirmed round onto his side. And then he froze.

There was a ghost in his room!

A shiver ran down every armoured plate on his back. Standing before him on four squat legs, a see-through kentrosaurus glowed eerie-green in the darkness.

"Arx!" shouted Teggs. "In here, quick!"

The ghost took a step closer. Flat, bony lumps lined the back of its neck. Two rows of twisted spines stretched from its back to its long, stiff tail. A fearsome spike jutted from each shoulder. Its head was small. Its eyes were wide and staring. Its toothless beak flapped open and shut like it was talking – but Teggs heard no words.

Then his door slid open and Arx came inside.

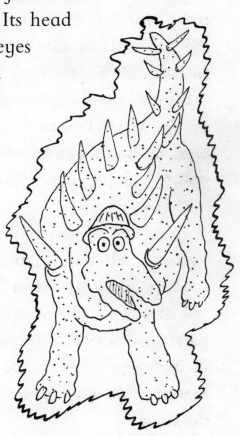

25

His green skin turned pale as the ghost turned to face him. Quickly he jabbed on the lights with one of his horns – and the vision vanished.

"I wasn't dreaming, was I?" Teggs demanded. "Did you see that thing?"

Arx sat down shakily. "I saw it all right. Did it hurt you?"

"No. But I wonder what it wanted . . ." Teggs looked at him grimly. "It seems Shanta was right. This place *is* haunted . . . by some kind of space ghost!"

Chapter Three

THE SECRET IN THE SAND

After his strange meeting with the
ghost, Teggs slept with the light on.

Arx did too.

Gipsy slept soundly through the
night, despite the mysterious noise from
the toilets.

27

As for Iggy, he was *in* the toilets –
and he hadn't slept a wink. The storm
had passed, the sun was starting to rise,
but still he worked on. He was
determined to stop the pipes from
rattling and
clunking.

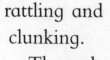

The only problem
was, he could find
nothing wrong
with them! The
noise seemed to
be coming from
deep down below.

Iggy sighed. If it
wasn't the pipes,
that meant there was a
blockage in the dung tanks – and he
didn't fancy diving through tons of
stinky muck to fix it.

Luckily, at that moment, Teggs came
in. "Come on, Iggy. I've called a
meeting with Shanta in the crew room."

28

Iggy saluted sleepily. But when Teggs told the tale of his ghostly visitor, he soon woke up.

"So, you've seen one too, my lad," said Shanta grimly. He looked at Arx. "Told you so!"

Gipsy shuddered. "I'm glad I only had noisy toilets to deal with!"

Teggs turned to Shanta. "Have the ghosts ever tried to hurt you or your miners?"

"Yes!" he said. "They hurt Herman, our best driller. He saw one and fell over – knocked one of his teeth out!"

Teggs shook his head. "That wasn't the ghost's fault! I mean, have they ever tried to harm you on purpose?"

"Well, no," said Shanta. "But they *are* very scary. Now you know why we need your help!"

"We can't do much about ghosts, can we?" asked Iggy.

Shanta shook his little head. "But you can help us find the dispium quickly so we can get off this horrid world! I will give the DSS half of whatever we find."

Arx's eyes lit up. "If dispium *does* exist, its mysterious powers could be very important for dinosaur science."

"I agree," said Teggs. "Of course we will help."

"But . . ." Iggy swallowed hard. "But what if dispium really *is* the cursed treasure? We don't want to end up haunting this place for ever like the kentrosaurus miners!"

"I don't believe in curses," Teggs told him.

"Arx didn't believe in ghosts until last night!" said Gipsy quietly. Then everyone jumped as her wrist communicator beeped loudly. "It's the dimorphodon!"

The dimorphodon were specially trained flying reptiles who worked the *Sauropod's* controls with their beaks and claws. There were fifty of them, and they were usually left in charge whenever Teggs and his chief officers were away.

Gipsy translated their squawks and chatter. "The dimorphodon were looking down at the planet from up in orbit, when they spotted something strange," she explained. "Looks like that big storm last night uncovered something buried in the sand . . . something big and metal and rusty."

Gipsy gasped. "They say it looks like part of a spaceship – just a few hundred metres from this camp!"

Shanta gasped. "Maybe it's the old kentrosaurus ship."

"The one in the old stories, that vanished as suddenly as the kentrosaurus did?" Teggs rubbed his hands together. "Let's take a look!"

Shanta woke up Herman and Frank, the other two miners, and they all trooped out into the cold sunlight.

Sure enough, just as the dimorphodon had said, the front of a spaceship was sticking out from a purple sand dune close by. Teggs and his team watched as the miners carefully dug it out with picks and shovels, holding the tools tightly with their peg-like teeth. Plod was working harder than any of them. She dug dementedly with a shovel, sending sand flying in all directions.

"That ship didn't just vanish," Arx murmured. "It was carried here and hidden on purpose!"

"How do you know?" asked Gipsy. "Maybe the sand just buried it over the years."

Iggy shook his head. "It's parked upside down! I suppose a big storm could have blown it over . . ."

"Not without damaging the ship," said Arx as Frank and Herman finished clearing away the sand. "And apart from some rust, it seems fine!"

"But who would want to hide it?" wondered Gipsy.

No one had a good answer.

"I'm not getting any closer," said Herman. "If that *is* the kentrosaurus ship, it could be cursed!"

34

"He's right!" said Frank.

Iggy's love of old spaceships overcame his fear. He jogged over and sniffed the engines. "Ah, yes. This ship ran on kentrosaurus dung all right. It's a very distinctive smell."

"I won't ask how he knows that!" said Teggs, grinning at Gipsy and Arx. "You two wait here. I'm going to look inside."

"Be careful, Captain," called Arx.

Teggs crept up to the old ship. Carefully, he hooked a tail spike over the door and pulled. The door creaked open. "Take this torch," said Shanta.

Teggs took it in his beak, and bravely went inside.

The ship was dead. Its power had drained away long ago. Teggs looked sadly at the empty control pit, at the withered ferns that the crew had never eaten. What terrible fate had befallen these long-lost dinosaurs? What drove their ghosts to roam on Creepus?

After a few minutes' poking about, Teggs's torch beam fell on a piece of paper lying on the floor. A map was marked on it. He pricked it with his tail and went back outside to show the others.

Iggy peered at the paper. "There's something written on the back. It says, 'Mine D here'." He frowned. "No sign of mines A, B and C though."

"Wait a moment!" cried Arx. "Mine D – that could be short for Mine *dispium* here!"

The dinosaurs gasped.

"This map might mark the very spot where the kentrosaurus made their discovery," said Teggs, smiling. "So – I reckon it's time for a mine hunt!"

Chapter Four

THE TREASURE TRAP

While Arx and Iggy searched the
spaceship for more clues, Teggs and
Gipsy set off with Shanta to look for
the mine.

Shanta knew the land around the camp
well, and soon worked out what the map
was showing. Teggs and Gipsy followed
him over plains of purple sand, across

38

marshy moors and through the foothills of mauve mountains. The sun glared down at them like an evil eye. A wild wind blew against them all the way. Then, as they approached the place marked on the map, it died away to nothing — like the weather itself was holding its breath.

"Don't forget, dispium is supposed to look like little red glowing cubes," Shanta told them. "Keep your eyes peeled."

Teggs and Gipsy gazed all around as they entered a gloomy gully.

Purple cliffs rose up sharply on either side of them, blocking out the sun.

And suddenly, in the shadows up ahead, the figures of four creepy kentrosaurus appeared.

"G-g-ghosts!" gasped Gipsy.

Shanta gulped. "I've never seen so many at once!"

The ghosts were glowing green. They reared up on their hind legs, swung their tails from side to side and opened their beaks in a silent scream . . .

"Don't be afraid," Teggs told his friends, though secretly even *he* was scared stiff. "I don't think they will hurt us. Back in the Stegosaur Sector where I grew up, the kentrosaurus had a reputation for being nice, kind people."

But even as he spoke, one of the
ghosts charged up to them and
waggled the spines on its back. Its beak
twisted open and it pawed the air like
it wanted to trample them.

"Are you sure?" Gipsy squeaked.
Then the other three ghosts ran
forwards, their shoulder spikes gleaming
in the gloom.

"Quick! Close your eyes and walk
straight through them!" Teggs
commanded.

41

"Walk *through* them?" Shanta stared at him. "You're bonkers!"

"No, he's brilliant!" cried Gipsy. "Ghosts aren't solid – so how can they harm us if they can't touch us?"

"Now!" Teggs shouted.

The spectres gave a silent gasp as he pushed through them! Gipsy and Shanta shut their eyes and followed.

For a moment, Gipsy felt very cold, like she had walked

through an icy shadow. Then she opened her eyes again and saw the ghosts were behind her. They looked confused.

"We did it!" laughed Shanta with relief. "We stood up to them and nothing happened!"

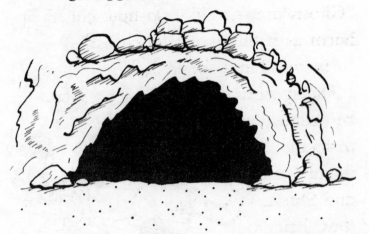

"And *that* must be the entrance to the mine," said Teggs. He headed over to a dark cave in the side of the cliff.

"Careful, Captain!" called Gipsy. Two of the ghosts had appeared on a ledge halfway up the cliff face. They were staring down at Teggs, still waving their tails.

"Ignore them," Teggs told her. "How can they bother us if they can't even touch us?"

But then
the whole cliff
started to rumble
and shake.
Seconds later,
huge rocks and
boulders started
tumbling down
from the
ledge where
the ghosts
were standing!

"Captain, look
out!" cried Gipsy.
"It's a rockfall!"

With no time to run, Teggs used his
tail to bat away the biggest ones. But
more and more were falling. One of
them was bound to squash him flat . . .

"Shanta, use your tail like a lasso,"
Gipsy shouted. "It's his only chance!"

"Reckon you're right, lassie," said
Shanta grimly. "Here goes!"

The diplodocus whipped his tail
around Teggs and yanked him clear
of the cave mouth — just as a pile of
purple rocks came pounding down on
the very spot he had been
standing on.

When the dust had settled, the cave
was sealed up by the fallen rocks and
the ghosts had gone. Teggs heaved a
sigh of relief. "Thanks, guys. I was
nearly a squished stegosaur!"

"And you were wrong about those
ghosts," said Shanta. "They *can* hurt us,
after all!"

"Hmm." Teggs was lost in thought. "I reckon there's more to these ghosts than meets the eye. How did they make the rocks fall if they can't touch anything?"

Gipsy scampered up the pile of freshly fallen rocks to investigate the ledge. There was a small machine there.

"Captain, I think this thing set off the rockfall," she called down. "Must be some sort of booby trap."

Shanta looked round nervously. "We should get out of here – before we set off another one!"

Teggs sighed. "I suppose so. Let's take the machine back with us and check it for clues. Then we can plan our next move . . ." He trailed off, staring at the ground. "Hey, what are they?"

Scattered among the chunks of rock were some strange blue jewels. They weren't dispium crystals.

They were perfectly round, like beautiful marbles.

Shanta stared at the round jewels in wonder. "In all my years of mining, I've never seen anything like this before!"

"Let's take them with us," said Teggs. "Maybe Arx will know what they are."

Quickly they gathered up the blue jewels and headed back to Camp Kentro. But they didn't see the ghosts watching them from the shadows with burning eyes . . .

Chapter Five

A ROAR IN THE DARK

Iggy, Arx and Plod were sitting in the crew room when Teggs, Gipsy and Shanta returned.

Arx was intrigued when they showed him the strange blue marbles. "Is there anywhere we can test them?"

"There's a small lab here," said Shanta. "Plod, could you show them where it is?"

"No problem. It's just by the toilets"
– Plod gave Iggy a look – "which are
still making funny sounds!"

"I haven't had time to fix them yet,"
Iggy protested. "I've been too busy
cleaning up the kentrosaurus ship."

"Find anything interesting?" asked
Teggs, helping himself to an extra-large
plate of plants.

"Yes!" said Iggy excitedly. "Did you
know, the engine was a Dungsmith
One Thousand? Worth a fortune!"

Teggs shook his head. "No, I mean,
did you find anything to do with
dispium, or what happened to the
kentrosaurus miners?"

"Er, no," Iggy admitted. "It was just
an ordinary ship. With the most
incredible engine! It had twenty-seven
gears, one for every—"

"Maybe these crystals can tell us
something," said Arx quickly. "I shall
start work on them right away!"

49

"What about this instant-rockfall maker?" asked Gipsy, holding up the strange machine. "Iggy, have you ever seen anything like it?"

"Nope." He opened it up with a screwdriver and peered inside. "Very clever, and very nasty. There's a special camera in here – it must have been pointed at one spot. I'll bet that when it saw you standing there for too long – *CRASH!* – it sent a shockwave into the cliff to start the rockfall."

"So the ghosts didn't start the rockfall after all," Teggs realized. "The machine was on automatic."

"I bet they set it when they were still alive," growled Shanta. "They wanted to keep all that dispium for themselves."

"And a lot of good it did them," sighed Gipsy.

"Greedy devils," said Shanta crossly. "They *still* want it all for themselves, even though they are ghosts. That's why they are trying to drive us away!"

"This is weird," said Iggy, dismantling the machine. "It's completely different technology to anything on board the kentrosaurus ship."

51

Teggs raised an eyebrow. "Then maybe it *doesn't* belong to the kentrosaurus. Maybe someone *else* has been skulking about on Creepus!"

"Or maybe the kentrosaurus just picked it up cheap at a spaceship-boot sale!" said Gipsy.

"I wish those ghosts could talk." Teggs sighed. "We need some proper answers."

Gipsy nodded. "If only it was safe to go back and explore that mine."

"It will be – if you hold on to this!" Iggy pulled out a circuit from the rockfall machine. "This is the bit that sends out shockwaves. If anything nasty comes after you, flick this switch and give it a shock!"

"That better not include me!" said Shanta. "I want to come with you."

Teggs shook his head. "Sorry, Shanta, you're just too big for a sneaky mission. The ghosts – or anyone else who might be watching – will see you coming for miles." He nibbled a leaf from his plate. "No, I had better go alone."

"If you're not back by midnight, we will come looking," Iggy promised.

Gipsy nodded. "Good luck, Captain."

It was getting dark by the time Teggs returned to the mine. He looked all around, carefully holding the shockwave maker in his beak. But there was no sign of life – or death, for that matter. The gulley was ghost-free.

53

Teggs crept up to the entrance of the mine, which was still blocked by tons of rock. He carefully aimed the shockwave maker and fired. The rocks jiggled like jelly, and then they blew apart! Luckily he was wearing his battle armour, and so the pieces just bounced off him.

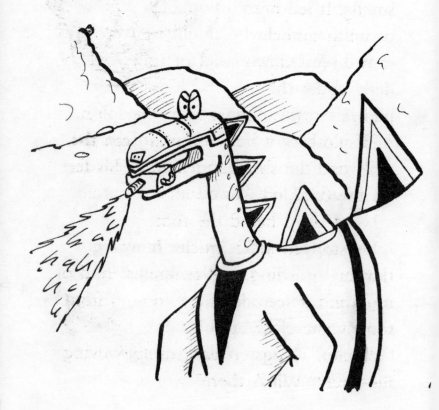

When the dust cleared, the black
mouth of the cave was open wide.
Teggs took a deep
breath, got out
Shanta's torch,
and went inside.

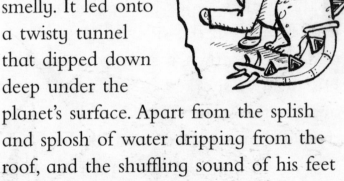

The cave was
damp and
smelly. It led onto
a twisty tunnel
that dipped down
deep under the
planet's surface. Apart from the splish
and splosh of water dripping from the
roof, and the shuffling sound of his feet
on the floor, all was quiet.

Until Teggs heard the roar.

He stopped in his tracks. It was a
throaty, growling, bad-tempered kind of
roar, and it seemed to be coming from
somewhere close by.

"Hello?" Teggs called bravely, waving
his torch. "Who's there?"

Suddenly a haze of green light
appeared ahead of him.

The ghosts were coming back!

Teggs backed away, looking for a
place to hide. He wanted to spy on
these ghosts up close. He was sure there
was more to them than met the eye . . .

Unfortunately, the same was true
of the tunnel. Teggs backed up into
a dark hole in the side of the wall –
and slipped down a steep, slimy slope.
His armour sparked as it scraped
against the stone. Then he fell
through empty space and landed with
a bump that took the
breath from his
body. A strange
red light
surrounded
him.

It was coming from the little red cubes of crystal all around him.

"Dispium!" he breathed. "Pure dispium!"

The crystals glowed with a mysterious, beautiful light. Teggs felt his eyes grow heavy and his body become light as a feather.

His head started spinning. "What's happening?" he gasped. The world around him was fading away. All he could see was the red, red glow . . .

And then everything went black.

Chapter Six

STRANGE MEETINGS

Back at Camp Kentro, in his well-lit lab, Arx was still testing the glowing blue marbles that Teggs and Gipsy had brought back from the ghostly gulley.

He had been at it for hours and hours, and had lost all track of time. Not even the strange noise from the nearby toilets could distract him – *Ratta-tatta-tatta-BZZZZZZZZ-CLUNK!*

The door slid open and Shanta's head snaked inside on the end of his long neck.

"Any news from Teggs?" Arx asked.

"He's not back yet," said Shanta. "It's close to midnight now, so Iggy and Gipsy have gone to look for him. How are you getting on with the marbles?"

Arx sighed wearily. "I've drilled them, chilled them, swilled them in acid and sliced them with lasers. But I still have absolutely no idea what they are or what they can do!"

"Maybe they just look pretty," Shanta suggested.

"I'm not giving up yet," said Arx. "Maybe if I *heat* them . . ." He put one in a clamp and placed it over a hot flame. "Oh, I do hope Iggy and Gipsy turn up with the captain soon . . ."

The marble gave off a tiny trail of blue smoke, and Arx shuffled forwards to study it. Then suddenly, from out of nowhere, a kentrosaurus appeared!

This one did not glow eerily like the ghosts they had seen. It looked solid

and real. "Stop them!" cried the kentrosaurus.

Arx gasped. "This one can talk!"

The dinosaur reared up on his back legs, and Shanta desperately dodged aside. "Beware!" the newcomer cried. "Beware the—"

But his words were lost as Shanta's snaking neck bumped into Arx's workbench. The experiments were sent flying. The flame went out and the heated marble splashed into a glass of water.

And the kentrosaurus vanished as quickly as it had appeared.

"I've never seen a ghost like *that* before," whispered Shanta, his enormous knees knocking together with fright.

"No," said Arx thoughtfully as he started to clear up the mess. "Neither have I . . ."

Teggs woke up in a dark cave, lit only by a flickering lamp. His brain felt like it had been boiled in hot mud. A kentrosaurus was watching him closely.

But this one was *not* a ghost. It looked gruff and solid and real – if a little bit grey about the scales. A miner's helmet was perched on its little head.

"We tried to stop you," said the dinosaur, "but you fell into a seam of pure dispium."

Teggs scrambled to his feet, still feeling dizzy. "You can speak!"

"I've always been able to speak. The difference is, you can hear me now."

The dinosaur sighed. "My name's Spink, Chief Miner."

"I've seen you before!" Teggs realized. "You scared me in my bedroom last night at Camp Kentro."

"*My* bedroom, you mean!" Spink retorted, and then he sighed again. "I like to go there to see the picture of Shirley on the wall. You know, it's been fifty years since I last saw her."

"But why? Why have you stayed in hiding all this time?" Teggs demanded. "And why are you trying to scare away the diplodocus miners?"

"We're not!" Spink protested.

"Come off it," snorted Teggs. "You've been making them think there are ghosts on this planet. You don't want them getting any dispium – but why? Surely there's enough for all of you?"

"You don't understand," said Spink sadly. "We haven't been trying to scare you. We've been trying to *warn* you!"

"Warn us?" Teggs frowned. "About what?"

"About coming near the dispium, of course!" Spink replied. "It's not called the cursed treasure for nothing. When we first found those little red crystals, we jumped for joy! What we *didn't* know was that they soon turn you completely see-through! No one can see us, or hear us, or touch us . . .

we might as *well* be ghosts!"

"Pull the other one, it's got moss on it!" Teggs snapped. "You are as solid as I am!"

"Yes, I'm afraid that's true," said Spink, rather strangely. "Like I said, we tried our best to keep you away . . ."

"By dropping a mountain on our heads!"

"That machine isn't ours," Spink told him. "We tried to show it to you, so you would realize the danger you were in!"

"I don't believe a word you're saying." Teggs looked at his watch and gasped. "It's well past midnight! My crew will be very worried about me. I must get back to them." He advanced on Spink. "And I should warn you, I'm going to tell them everything."

"You will find that much harder than you think." Spink stood aside for him. "Come on, then, the exit is this way."

Teggs frowned. "Aren't you going to try and stop me?"

Spink shook his head.

Feeling uneasy, Teggs followed him out of the mine. In the moonlight, at the far end of the gully, he saw Iggy and Gipsy. They were looking extremely worried.

"Guys!" he shouted. "It's all right, I'm here!"

But Iggy and Gipsy ignored him. They turned their backs. They seemed to be searching for something.

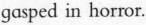

"What's wrong?" he called, running up to them.

"I can't see Captain Teggs anywhere," said Gipsy, like he wasn't there.

"Stop messing around," said Teggs. "I have to tell you something!"

Then Iggy turned round – and gasped in horror. "Look, Gipsy – the captain!"

Gipsy did – and her jaw dropped in horror. "Oh, *no*!"

Teggs was bewildered. "What in space is the matter with you two?"

But Teggs couldn't see himself the way that Gipsy and Iggy did. To them he was a transparent figure, glowing eerie-green in the night.

To them, he looked exactly like a space ghost!

Chapter Seven

BLAST FROM THE PAST!

"Poor Captain Teggs," Gipsy sniffed.
"The dispium has cursed him too. He's
just the same as the old kentrosaurus
miners!"

"We must tell
Arx right away,"
said Iggy,
wiping a tear
from his eye.
"Come on."

"Wait!" Teggs
yelled as they
rushed away
from him.
"Don't go!"

"I tried to tell you," said Spink, waddling up beside him. "You have changed, Teggs. Now, to anyone who has *not* been near dispium, you can only be glimpsed in the dark as a spooky, see-through green phantom. And they can't hear you at all."

"But it's not fair!" grumbled Teggs. "I'm too young to be a ghost."

"I've been a ghost for fifty years now." Spink scowled. "It's rubbish! Other ghosts can see and touch you, but no one else. It gets ever so lonely. We long to fly our ship back home – but being ghosts we can't hold the controls!"

70

Teggs patted his shoulder. "I'm sorry I didn't believe you. You really *were* trying to warn us."

"And not just about the dispium," said Spink gravely. "There are evil creatures at work on Creepus. They have been here for years. They hid our spaceship so no one would come looking for us and our maps so no one could find the mine. And they set the rockfall trap, just in case. *They* don't want anyone near the dispium either – but for a very different reason."

"Did they make that scary roar I heard?" Teggs asked.

"No, that was their pet monster, looking for lunch." Spink shuddered. "They call it . . . the kraggle-scruncher."

"The *what*?"

"The kraggle-scruncher! So named because if it finds you, it scrunches you into a kraggle and eats you!"

Teggs wasn't sure what a kraggle was, but it sounded painful.

"You were heading straight for it," Spink went on. "We wanted to warn you away — but then you fell."

Teggs nodded gloomily. "Who *are* these evil creatures and what are they up to?"

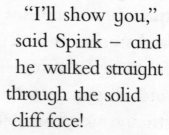

"I'll show you," said Spink — and he walked straight through the solid cliff face!

Teggs stared. "I can't follow you that way."

"Course you can! It's easy when you know how." Spink stuck his head back out. "When you were solid you could walk through us ghosts, remember? Well, now you're a ghost you can walk through anything solid! Just close your eyes and do it — but try not to sink into the ground!"

Teggs took a deep breath and gave it a try. Spink was right, it *was* easy! He walked straight through the cliff face like it wasn't there, and followed the miner through the dark rock.

Deeper and deeper they went, through tunnels and caves and storerooms, all filled to the brim with dispium or the strange blue marbles.

Then Teggs heard a familiar noise somewhere close by: *RATTA-TATTA-BZZZZZZZZZZZ-tatta-CLUNK!*

"That's the sound of the toilets in Camp Kentro!" he realized.

Spink shook his head. "It's not, you know. It's the sound of a big loading machine *beneath* the toilets! The ground under our old base is totally hollow now. Every last cube of dispium is being removed . . ."

Teggs stamped his foot in frustration. "If only we could tell Shanta and the others!"

"What do you think we've been trying to do!" Spink told him.

Slowly, the tunnels grew hotter and brighter, filled with the fiery glow of the cursed crystals.

"Not far now," said Spink. "We must be very careful. They mustn't find us!"

"*Who* mustn't find us?" asked Teggs tetchily. But then Spink led him to the mouth of an enormous cavern and he saw for himself.

Nimble, nasty little creatures were working in the cavern. Some carried picks and shovels. Some used powerful drills. Others pushed trolleys full of dispium crystals. Their hides were striped orange and black. Their mouths were crammed with vicious teeth. Their cold yellow eyes flickered this way and that as they scurried about.

"Raptors!" breathed Teggs in disbelief. "*Raptors*, here in the heart of the Vegetarian Sector! Are they ghosts too?"

"These ones are," Spink whispered. "But the raptors aren't stuck the way we are. They have found a way to reverse the process."

"That's wonderful news!" said Teggs excitedly. "Maybe *we* can get back to normal too. How do they do it?"

"We don't know!" said Spink. "Every time we try to get close enough to find out, the kraggle-scruncher comes after us."

Teggs was puzzled. "But if you're ghosts, how can it hurt you?"

"The kraggle-scruncher has been specially bred to scrunch *anything*, whether it's see-through or solid," Spink informed him.

76

"And it loves to hunt. That's the only reason the raptors haven't killed us for real — we make good sport for their perishing pet."

Teggs sighed. "Well, at least things can't get any worse!"

But, almost at once, they did.

A big, scaly raptor in a tight black uniform strolled into sight. His whole head was scuffed and scraped. One eye was hidden by a black patch but the other gleamed with sly cunning.

"Faster, you fools!" he hissed. "Every last cube of crystal must be collected! Soon we will leave this dump for ever . . . and put our evil plans into action!"

"Oh, *no!*" groaned Teggs. "Not *him!*"

Spink frowned. "You know him?"

"That's General Loki — the most dangerous raptor in the universe. A ghost from my past." Teggs slapped his forehead. "Except *I'm* the ghost, aren't I! Whatever Loki's up to . . . how can I possibly hope to stop him now?"

Then suddenly an ear-splitting roar sounded behind them.

Teggs whirled round to find a terrifying monster was approaching. It glowed like a ghost but it was as solid as rock — a huge, green spiky ball with a huge, red spiky mouth and huge, white spiky teeth. A muscly arm sprouted from its top and ended in a fat fist. The monster hopped along on one gigantic foot with sixteen toes. On each toe was a bloodshot eyeball, staring at them with hatred.

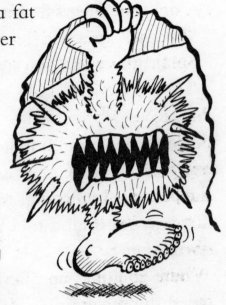

"It's the kraggle-scruncher!" hissed Spink. "It has hunted us down!"

A ball of white fire burst from the kraggle-scruncher's mouth and exploded at their feet. Teggs gulped as the monster hopped forwards to get them . . .

Chapter Eight

LAST LAUGH TO LOKI?

Back above ground, Iggy and Gipsy had returned to Camp Kentro. They called Arx, Shanta and the others to the crew room and told them their terrible news.

"The captain is a ghost," said Iggy quietly. "I'm afraid . . . he must be dead!"

Arx's horns drooped like melted candles. He couldn't take it in.

"It's the curse!" cried Plod. "Teggs has been got by the curse!" Frank and Herman clung to each other in fear.

"I can't bear to think of him haunting this horrible planet for ever," sobbed Gipsy. Arx gave her a hug.

"That does it," said Shanta firmly. "Dispium or no dispium, we must leave this place and never come back – or the curse will get us as well!" He stood up, almost banging his head on the roof.

"Come on, lads. We'll get to our own base, grab the others and get the ship ready for take-off."

Plod dipped her neck down to the astrosaurs' level. "I'm sorry," she told them. Then she followed her fellow miners from the room.

The astrosaurs stood alone in gloomy silence.

"Are you absolutely *sure* Captain Teggs was a ghost?" asked Arx.

"He was all green and glowing," said Iggy.

"And he was speaking to us, but we couldn't hear a word," Gipsy added.

"I wonder . . ." Arx looked at them both. "Shanta and I saw a ghost tonight too. Or rather, a *kind-of* ghost. It appeared in the brightly-lit lab instead of in the dark. It was normal and solid. It even spoke to us before it disappeared!"

Gipsy stared at him in surprise. "What did it say?"

"'Stop them' and 'Beware'."

"Stop who?" wondered Iggy. "*Beware* who?"

"I don't know." Arx sighed. "It might have said more, except Shanta knocked over my experiment then, and it vanished. Even so, it's got me thinking . . ."

"Go on," Gipsy urged him.

Arx looked at them both. "Maybe the ghosts on Creepus aren't really ghosts at all. Maybe they are . . . something else!"

"Like what?" asked Gipsy excitedly.

"I don't know," Arx admitted.

"You're just trying to make us feel better," said Iggy.

"Well, one thing is for sure," said Arx. "We're not ready to run out on our captain, whatever's happened to him – right?"

"Right," Iggy and Gipsy declared.

"So let's go back to my lab and see if the kind-of ghost comes back," said Arx. "I only hope it can answer some of our questions!"

None of the astrosaurs could have known that, far beneath their feet, their captain was still very much alive.

But for how much longer?

The fearsome kraggle-scruncher was hopping towards Teggs and Spink.

"Swing your tail with mine!" Teggs ordered. "We'll hit him together. One – two – *three*!"

WHUCK! Two spiked and bony
tails struck the kraggle-scruncher right
in the kisser. It rolled over like a ball –
then bounced off the wall and charged
after them on its single foot.

"You could say it's hopping mad!"
cried Teggs.

"Quick," Spink hissed. "Through the
wall!"

Teggs shut his eyes and followed Spink
through the solid rock – but this was
no obstacle to the kraggle-scruncher.
It glowed bright yellow for a moment
and bounded straight after them.

They came out into another tunnel. "Let's try down here," said Teggs, leading the way.

But they ran smack into a rabble of ghost-raptors carrying crates full of dispium.

"Ssstop them! Ssslash them!" The raptors threw down their crates and swiped at the dinosaurs with razor-sharp claws. Teggs and Spink dodged through another wall and into a different tunnel.

But they could still hear the kraggle-scruncher, hard on their heels – and now, hard on *its* heel, was the pack of raptors!

"If only we could get up above and try to warn my crew!" Teggs panted.

"We mustn't!" puffed Spink. "We would lead the kraggle-scruncher straight to them!"

They ran on, through solid rock and gloomy tunnels until their lungs were bursting. Then suddenly they found themselves in another huge underground cavern.

RATTA-TAT-BZZZZZZ-CRUNCH!
Now Teggs could see the cause of the racket in Camp Kentro's toilets with his own eyes. A big machine with metal claws was scooping dispium from a crate and dumping it inside the biggest raptor death ship he had ever seen. The craft filled the cavern like an enormous fang.

"Let's hide in there," gasped Teggs. "There might be something we can fight with!"

They dashed straight through the wall of the ship. Half the rooms were already filled with dispium. The others were stacked high with the strange blue marbles.

"They have been mining for years," said Spink. "Now they are ready to take their haul away."

Teggs nodded. "But what do they need the blue marbles for?"

"Wouldn't *you* like to know?" came a silky-soft whisper.

General Loki was standing right behind them!

Teggs turned to face his old enemy and his eyes narrowed. "You."

"Correct!" The evil raptor chuckled. "Me! Commander of the Seven Fleets of Death! Ruler of the meat mines of Raptos! Killer of kentrosaurus, eater of—"

"Talk to the tail, mister," said Teggs, turning away. "Quick, Spink, run!"

"Too late, pea-brain!" sneered Loki.

Teggs froze as ghost-raptors rushed through the death ship's walls and surrounded them. And a blood-curdling roar told Teggs that the kraggle-scruncher was just outside, waiting.

"I have a score to settle with you, Captain." Loki's single eye glinted. "When we last met, your stupid spaceship blasted me all the way to Planet Sixty. The place was full of T. rexes! I had to feed them my entire crew before they would let me go!"

"You heartless monster!" Teggs scowled. "What are you up to here?"

"I am in the business of *war*!" hissed Loki. "And unlike you and those kentrosaurus saps, *I* can completely control the effects of dispium! The boys and I can make ourselves silent, invisible ghosts whenever we choose – and change back to normal again just as quickly."

"Show-off," grumbled Teggs.

"Think about it, Captain." Loki showed his pointy teeth in an evil grin. "I can turn an entire army of raptors into space ghosts. No one will be able to see us in daylight so thousands of us can creep into any city we like – then turn ourselves solid and take over!"

Spink gulped. "You will be able to invade any planet you like and no one will even notice – until it's too late!"

"Precisely," said Loki. "We can kidnap kings . . . rob banks . . . feed on thousands of plant-eaters . . . anything we want!" He threw back his scaly head and laughed. "The entire Jurassic Quadrant will fall to our invisible might. Soon I, General Loki, will hold the whole galaxy in my jaws!"

Chapter Nine

A GHOST OF A CHANCE

Back in Arx's lab, the astrosaurs were twiddling their thumbs, waiting for the kind-of ghost to come back. All except  Arx, who didn't actually have any thumbs. He just wiggled his horns a bit.

They had been waiting most of the night.

"I wonder if Shanta has got his spaceship ready yet," said Gipsy.

"Soon it'll just be the three of us left here." Iggy sighed, folding his arms.

"We could be sitting around for weeks. It's driving me crazy! If I don't do something soon, I reckon I'll lose my marbles!"

Then the funny noise started up again from the toilets. *BZZZZ-CLUNK-ratta-tatta-BZZZZZZ!*

"That's what I'll do — fix that stupid noise," he declared. "It's getting right up my snout!"

Gipsy sighed as he stamped out of the room. Then Arx started staring hard at the experiments on his bench. "Marbles," he breathed. "Lose my marbles . . ."

"Oh, Arx, not you too!" Gipsy groaned.

"No! I mean *these* marbles!" He kicked some of the strange blue stones. "I was just running another test on them when the kind-of ghost

94

appeared. And when Shanta smashed the experiment, the kind-of ghost vanished again."

"You think those marbles affect the ghosts in some way?" Gipsy was gripped by sudden excitement. "Turn off the lights, Arx. The ghosts have only ever been seen in the dark, remember?"

Frowning, he did as she said. Suddenly, in the darkness, a creepy green kentrosaurus appeared. Another stood behind it. And another. They waved their arms urgently at the astrosaurs, swung their tails and yelled silently.

"I . . . I think they want our help," whispered Gipsy. She turned the lights back on. "Quickly, Arx. What were you doing with the marbles when the kind-of ghost appeared?"

"Oh dear!" Arx scratched his frilly head. "I can't remember!"

"But you must!" said Gipsy. "You *must*!"

Down in the death ship, General Loki had grown bored with showing off about his evil plans. To liven things up and to amuse his miners, he decided he would throw Teggs and Spink to the kraggle-scruncher!

The raptors shoved their captives out through the side of the ship to where the hideous monster was waiting. Then they stood in a big circle around the walls of the cavern so Teggs and Spink could not escape.

The kraggle-scruncher hopped up and down with pleasure at the sight of its victims. Its eyes narrowed on every toe. It opened its massive mouth and belched a ball of fire right at them.

Teggs and Spink jumped up in the air. The flames whooshed underneath them and singed their soles.

"What are we going to do?" cried Spink.

"I'll think of something," Teggs gasped, dodging a blow from the kraggle-scruncher's mighty arm. "You mustn't give up hope!"

The raptors around them jeered and cheered. They were so excited that none of them noticed when some rubble and a pile of dung balls fell down from the roof . . .

Iggy was angry, upset and up to his ears in dung. To take his mind off his misery he had taken up the floor in the toilets and opened up the dung tanks, determined to find and stop the nuisance noise. But now he could hear something else. Something far stranger.

It sounded like a massive monster was hopping about on one big foot right beneath him, breathing fire in all directions.

So Iggy kept digging down through the dung. It was stale and hard, like tunnelling through smelly rock, but he kept on going. Finally, in his anger, he put his pick through the bottom of the dung tank – and right through the rock.

Iggy realized he had made himself a spyhole. He bent over to look and gasped. He didn't believe what he was seeing!

There *was* a massive monster hopping about on one big foot right beneath him and breathing fire in all directions! And ringed around it in spooky silence were a hundred ravenous raptors, glowing like ghosts in the darkness. And there, looking equally ghostly as they tried to escape the monster, were Teggs and a kentrosaurus!

Iggy knew he had to get Arx and Gipsy. But then, to his horror, he realized he was stuck in the bottom of the hole he had dug. The sides were too steep to climb back out!

And through the spyhole he could see that Teggs and his friend were in deadly danger. The monster's blows and its fire were coming closer and closer . . .

Spink wasn't as quick as Teggs, and the kraggle-scruncher finally got him. Its monstrous knuckles bashed him right in the beak, and he rolled over and over. He came to rest beside a big pile of the blue marbles waiting to be loaded onto the ship, and lay still. The raptors jeered and laughed.

"Spink, are you OK?" Teggs tugged on his shoulder spike. "Get up!"

The kraggle-scruncher hopped towards them, bellowing in triumph.

"I wonder what you'll taste like toasted, Teggs," gloated General Loki. "I think I'm about to find out!"

The monster's huge mouth was opening. A fireball was forming there.

"Now, Spink!" Teggs thundered. "You have to get *up*!"

But the kentrosaurus was too groggy to react.

WHOOOSH!

The fireball launched from the kraggle-scruncher's throat.

At the last moment, with all his strength, Teggs hurled his friend aside.

The fireball struck
the mound of blue
marbles with a
fiery blast.
They burst
into bright
blue flames.
Smoke
swamped
Teggs and
Spink, making them sneeze.

"No!" shouted Loki. "You blundering
monster!"

"What's rattled the raptor?" asked
Spink weakly.

"I . . . I don't know," said Teggs. He
felt suddenly strange — dizzy and dazed
and definitely different . . . "Wait a
minute!" He nudged one smoking
marble with his beak and it rolled
away. "Spink, did you see that?" he
gasped. "I can touch things! I'm not a
ghost any more! Spink, *you* try it!"

Spink whacked his tail into the marble pile, bombarding the kraggle-scruncher with blazing stones. It howled with pain and the smoke gave it a nasty coughing fit. "Me too!" cried Spink. "I'm my old self again!"

"It must be that smoke! It's turned us back to normal!" Teggs swung round to face General Loki. "So *that's* why you've been mining the blue stones! When they burn, they give off a special smoke that reverses the effects of the dispium!"

For a moment, Loki and the raptors seemed to fade away like ghosts. Only their green outlines were left behind, glowing in the gloom. But  then they turned solid again.

"You are quite correct, Captain," hissed Loki. "With a good supply of blue marbles and dispium, we can turn see-through or solid as we choose. But the knowledge will do you no good. My pet can hunt anyone, ghostly or not. And it is high time you were scrunched to a kraggle!"

The kraggle-scruncher coughed up a ferocious fireball that knocked the plant-eaters right off their feet. The raptors cheered.

"Enjoy yourself while you can, Loki," said Teggs fearlessly. "Pride has been known to come before a fall."

And what a fall it was!

Two seconds later, a large and smelly iguanodon fell with a yell through the roof above them. He landed with a stinky splat, right on top of the kraggle-scruncher – squashing it flat!

"Whew," said the steaming, dung-covered dinosaur. "Thank goodness for a soft landing!"

"Iggy!" beamed Teggs. "You saved us."

Iggy grinned back. "Sorry I couldn't have a bath first."

"You astrosaur beasts!" General Loki was red with rage. "You squished my pet monster!"

Teggs nodded happily. "I do believe he's been scrunched to a kraggle himself!"

Loki's eye narrowed. "That will seem like paradise next to what we're going to do to you . . ."

He and his raptors closed in on them, their talons raised.

Chapter Ten

FRIGHTS AND FIGHTS AND
FINAL FLIGHTS

"Never mind, Captain," said Iggy bravely. "We can't beat all these raptors, but at least we'll go down fighting!"

"*We* can't beat them," said Teggs, pulling a small device from his belt, "but maybe the roof will! Because now we're back in the solid world again, I can use *this*."

Iggy grinned. "The shockwave maker!"

"Cover your heads!" cried Teggs as he fired the shockwave maker at the roof. The rock trembled like a trifle in a typhoon, and then broke apart.

"Er, Captain?" said Iggy. "The dung tanks are up there!"

But they weren't for long.

With a loud squelch, tons of dung fell down from the shattered ceiling. The raptors yelped and gurgled as the stinky brown muck knocked them to the ground. But it covered Teggs, Spink and Iggy too, and knocked the shockwave maker from the captain's beak.

"Where's General Loki?" asked Teggs, pushing his head out from the dung heap. "Did we get him?"

"No, you did not, Captain!" shouted Loki. He and his best troops had reached the safety of their spaceship just in time. "And since you seem to be stuck, there's nothing to stop us biting your boring heads right off!"

"Nothing, you say?" Teggs smiled. "What about *them*?"

The shockwave maker had left a huge hole in the cavern roof – or in other words, a huge hole in the floor of the Camp Kentro toilets. Now a pair of kentrosaurus came into view, sturdy and solid. At once, they jumped down and started to battle Loki's best raptors.

Another kentrosaurus
swiftly followed to
join in the fight.
And then another,
and another . . .

"My boys!"
gasped Spink.
"They . . . they're
not ghosts any more. They are normal
again! But they weren't near the
smoke, so how . . . ?"

"Ask *him*," said Teggs, nodding at the
delighted triceratops peering at them
through the hole.

"Captain, you seem quite your old
self!" beamed Arx. "It's remarkable. I
burned some of the marbles you found
in the rockfall and they gave off this
blue smoke. It's turned all the
kentrosaurus ghosts back to normal!"

"You see, Loki?" Teggs hollered. "Now
Arx has learned your secret too —
worst luck for you!"

110

"This isn't fair!" cried Loki. "Curse you, astrosaurs!"

Teggs shook his head. "The curse of the dispium is ended, Loki," he said triumphantly. "Along with your plans to conquer the universe."

The old miners fought furiously, using their shoulder spikes and tails to wipe the floor with the raptors.

"Your boys are good fighters," said Iggy admiringly.

"They've been watching the raptors helplessly for years," said Spink. "Now at last they can fight back!"

"We sssurrender," hissed a battered raptor as it flopped face-first in the dung. The kentrosaurus cheered.

"It's not over yet," said Teggs, finally freeing himself from the muck heap. "We've got to stop Loki for good. Let's get aboard that death ship, fast."

"Too late!" The evil raptor was leaning out of the window of his death ship. "You may have beaten my troops, but I've still got all the dispium and the blue marbles I need to build another invisible army. You'll never know where we'll strike next!"

The kentrosaurus retreated as Loki fired up the engines. Then the death ship used its lasers to blast a hole in the cavern wall, revealing a large shaft sloping upwards towards the surface.

"Those sneaky raptors built a secret launch chute," gasped Iggy. "Loki's going to smash his way out."

"If he does, the shockwaves could flatten Camp Kentro!" Spink yelled.

The engines roared like a million kraggle-scrunchers with cramp in their toes — and the death ship took off up the launch chute at incredible speed.

"Arx," yelled Teggs. "Get everyone out of Camp Kentro, *quick*!"

"Nobody's *in* the camp, Captain," Arx called down. "Shanta and his miners have left the planet."

"Not quite, Arx," said Gipsy, appearing just behind him with a huge smile on her face. "I've just called them on my communicator . . ."

There was an ear-splitting crash as the death ship burst through the ground. Gipsy and Arx clung to each other as the tremors rocked Camp Kentro. The walls wobbled. Windows broke. The ceiling cracked open like an enormous eggshell to reveal the purple sky . . .

Where the biggest spaceship Teggs had ever seen was hovering right above the camp!

"That's a diplodocus ship," cried Iggy.

Gipsy nodded. "It's Shanta's. I called him once the kentrosaurus turned back to normal and told us what was going on. He said he'd stick around in his ship in case he could help."

"I only hope he can!" Teggs murmured.

They watched tensely as Loki's craft zoomed into view.

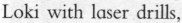

A split-second later, Shanta's ship opened fire on Loki with laser drills, mine missiles and dung torpedoes. Loki was so surprised that he forgot to put up his shields! The death ship burst into flames and dive-bombed down to the planet's surface.

"Quick," Teggs cried, turning to Iggy and the kentrosaurus miners. "Let's climb out of here and find out what's happened. Loki's a slippery customer. He might have got away."

Together they all crawled and climbed and slipped and slithered over the whiffy rock until they reached the big hole. Arx and Gipsy helped them out. Then, panting for breath, they ran through the remains of Camp Kentro. Finally, they stumbled outside.

Shanta had parked his craft beside the burning death ship, and now he was smiling down at them.

"Looking for someone?"

There, pinned to the ground by one of Plod's enormous feet, was General Loki.

"Well, well." Teggs grinned.

"The boot's on the other foot now, isn't it, Loki? And *what* a foot!"

"You can't treat me like this, you hopeless herbivores!" screeched the raptor. "I'm General Loki! Commander of the Seven Fleets of Death! Ruler of the meat mines of—"

"Oh, put a sock in it," said Teggs.

"I liked him better when he was a

ghost," added Iggy. "Couldn't hear a thing he was saying!"

"Well, I'm sure Admiral Rosso and the DSS will want to listen to every word of his confession," said Arx sternly. "Loki, you are going to be locked up for a very long time."

"While we are *free* again!" beamed Spink. "After all these years, I can finally go home and see Shirley."

"You certainly can," said Gipsy. "Your spaceship is as good as new – Iggy's fixed it up a treat."

The kentrosaurus cheered and raised Iggy up onto their shoulders. "It was a pleasure, boys!" he told them. "In fact, I wouldn't mind going for a spin in it myself!" He laughed as Spink and the others carried him off, cheering and whooping for joy.

Shanta smiled. "And now that you have learned the secret of dispium, Teggs, we can mine it properly!"

But Teggs shook his head. "No, Shanta. I don't think that's wise. If another villain like Loki ever got their hands on it, it really *would* be a cursed treasure. A weapon like that is just too dangerous."

"I think the DSS should put a force field around the whole planet, like an enormous protective bubble," said Gipsy. "Then no one can ever land here again."

"Good idea," Teggs agreed. "We should let Creepus keep its secrets."

Shanta sighed. "I suppose you're right."

"Why not take some of the blue marbles away with you instead?" Arx suggested. "After all, they make beautiful gemstones."

"That's true," said Plod. "We could sell them and make a fortune!"

"So everyone's a winner," grinned Teggs. Then he looked down at Loki. "Well – *almost* everyone."

"I just hope this particular space ghost never haunts us again!" said Gipsy.

"You will pay for spoiling my plans," moaned Loki, wriggling in the grip of Plod's toes. Then he accidentally swallowed a mouthful of sand, which finally shut him up.

Gipsy smiled at Teggs. "I'm so glad you're back to normal, Captain."

"So am I," said Teggs. "But you know, there was one good thing about being a ghost."

"There was?" asked Arx. "What?"

"I couldn't feel my stomach – so I didn't realize how hungry I was." He licked his lips. "Right now, I could eat a medium-sized forest!"

Gipsy laughed. "Then let's round up the rest of the raptors stuck down in the dung-heap and get back to the *Sauropod* for some breakfast. The dimorphodon will be wondering what's happened to us."

"They will never believe it," said Arx.

"I can hardly believe it myself," Gipsy admitted.

"But that's the brilliant thing about adventures, isn't it?" Teggs grinned. "*Anything* can happen. And I can't wait for it to happen to us again, very soon!"

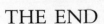

THE END

ASTRO PUZZLE TIME

THE SPACE GHOSTS
QUIZ Questions

1. What snacks did Shanta and Plod offer the crew upon their arrival at Camp Kentro?

2. What is the mysterious power of dispium crystals?

3. Why did the ghost of Spink often return to his old bedroom?

4. How many toes did the kraggle-scruncher have?

5. What was Arx doing to the marbles when the kentrosaurus appeared?

Answers:

5. Heating them.

4. Sixteen.

3. To gaze at the picture of his beloved Shirley on the wall.

2. They turn people into living ghosts.

1. Swamp tea and fried ferns.

ASTRO PUZZLE TIME

GHOST OF A CHANCE!

Uh-oh! Looks like the people and things below have been sitting too close to dispium crystals! Can you identify them from their outlines alone?

1.

2.

3.

4.

Answers:

1.Tegus 2.the *Saurepod* 3.General Loki 4.Kragle-Scruncher

ASTROSAURS
BOOK SEVEN

DAY OF THE
DINO-DROIDS

Read the first chapter here!

Chapter One

THE TUNNEL IN SPACE

Captain Teggs was
a very worried
dinosaur.

Most days, he
felt on top of
the world – on
top of any world.
After all, he was in
charge of the DSS

Sauropod, the best ship in the whole Dinosaur Space Service. But today, sat in the Sauropod's control pit, he was worried. And with good reason. Admiral Rosso had disappeared.

"I've double-checked the admiral's movements," said Arx, Teggs's second-in-command, looking up from his controls. "He left in his private starship for a holiday on the planet Trimuda. But no one has seen or heard from him since."

Teggs nodded glumly. "And he was due back at DSS HQ yesterday!" He turned to his communications officer, a stripy hadrosaur named Gipsy. "Anything to report?"

"I've listened in to every message sent and every signal received in Trimuda's part of space over the last week." Gipsy put down her headphones with a sigh. "Nothing from Admiral Rosso."

Teggs chewed on some bracken. "I just hope we find him safe and well – and fast. The Pick-a-Planet meeting is due to be held in just three days, and if we're not back at DSS HQ with Admiral Rosso by then . . ."

"It could mean trouble," said Gipsy.

"Trouble with a capital T!" Teggs agreed.

New planets were discovered at the outer edges of the Jurassic Quadrant all the time. If they were found in the Vegetarian Sector, they were claimed by the plant-eaters. If they were found in the Carnivore Sector, they were taken by the meat-eaters. But any worlds discovered close to the Vegmeat Zone – the no-man's land between the two dinosaur empires – were up for grabs. And each side wanted these worlds for themselves.

In olden times, there would be a big battle for each of the planets. But now, thanks to Admiral Rosso, things were different. Meat-eaters and plant-eaters alike gathered each year at DSS HQ for the Pick-a-Planet meeting. Here, the battles were fought with words, not weapons, and the planets were divided up evenly.

But Rosso was the only dinosaur trusted by both sides to play fair. Without him, the meeting could go dangerously wrong . . .

A loud bleep made the astrosaurs jump.

Gipsy frowned at her controls. "It's Iggy," she said. "He's sent a code-two warning signal."

"What?" Teggs reared up in his control pit. "Put him on screen!"

Iggy's face appeared on the scanner.
"Captain, the engines seem to be playing up. I can't stop the ship slipping sideways through space!"

"Sideways?" Teggs frowned. "What do your controls say, Arx?"

"Iggy's right. We are drifting off-course."

"But why?" Gipsy wondered.

Arx looked very serious. "Something is pulling us towards it!"

"Let's see what's out there," said Teggs.

"Nothing but a few stars and empty blackness!" Gipsy declared.

"It may be blackness, but I don't

think it's empty." Arx turned to face his friends. "There's only one thing in space with the power to drag things towards it like this. A black hole!"

Teggs jumped out of his control pit. "A black hole? But that's the most dangerous thing in the universe. Once it starts to suck you in, there's no escape!"

Read the rest of
DAY OF THE DINO-DROIDS
to find out what's happened to
Admiral Rosso!

Visit www.**stevecolebooks**.co.uk for fun, games, jokes, to meet the characters and much, much more!

Welcome to a world where dinosaurs fly spaceships and cows use a time-machine . . .

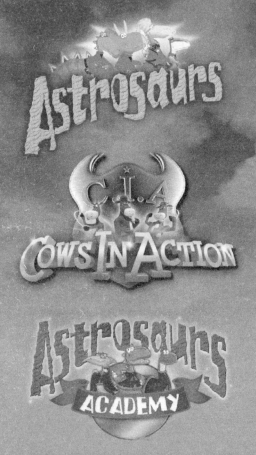

Sign up for the Steve Cole monthly newsletter to find out what your favourite author is up to!